THIS BLOOMSBURY BOOK

BELONGS TO

....

For everyone who's had a bad hair day – and Janine *MM*

For Joshua *LC*

BLOOMSBURY
CHILDREN'S
BOOKS

First published in Great Britain in 2003 by Bloomsbury Publishing Plc
38 Soho Square, London, W1D 3HB

This paperback edition first published in 2004

A CIP catalogue record of this book is available from the British Library
ISBN 0 7475 6482 5

Printed in China

3 5 7 9 10 8 6 4 2

All papers used by Bloomsbury Publishing are natural, recyclable products made from wood grown in well-managed forests.
The manufacturing processes conform to the environmental regulations of the country of origin.

Bad Hare Day

by Miriam Moss

illustrated by Lynne Chapman

BLOOMSBURY
CHILDREN'S
BOOKS

Herbert Hare was a hairdresser. The best in town.

Everyone came from miles around to be styled, sculpted, cut or conditioned by Herbert.

Inside his salon all was calm.
Soft music played, fans whirred
and the coffee machine hummed.

Clink! a chair was raised.

Snip! soft hair slithered to the ground.

Swish! the assistant swept it up.

"Now who's coming today?" said Herbert, looking in his book one March morning.

"A wash and blow dry for Bear,

a feathered cut
for Colobus,

a perm for Panda

and long layers for Llama."

"And that's just the beginning!" said Herbert happily,
throwing open the doors with a flourish.

On the pavement outside stood Holly, Herbert's niece.
"Hello," she said. "Mama says you're to look after me
while she goes shopping."
"Oh!" said Herbert. "I hope you'll be good."

Holly climbed on to a seat
and opened a magazine.
"I'm sure I shall," she said.

SNIP

While Herbert was busy brushing Bear's hair,
Holly helped herself to a drink.
First a cup of chocolate, then a raspberry milk,
then a herb tea, then a mixture of all three.

Chocolate

Herb Tea

Raspberry Milk

Coffee

Holly carried on playing with the buttons –
until the machine was completely empty.

"Shampoo delivery!" shouted a man
in overalls from the back door.

The Hare House

Herbert and his
assistant scurried off to
sort out the stock room.

While Herbert was away, Holly cleaned the mirrors
with fine sprays and chatted to the customers.
Then she adjusted the controls on the hood dryer.

The queue grew.

Helpful Holly sat everyone down in a row.
Then she went up and down,
shaving a neck here,

snipping a beard there

and fixing Bald
Eagle's new wig.

Holly bleached out
Badger's stripes

and gave
Orang Utan
a terribly
tight perm.

Llama wanted
long layers,
but she got a
short fringe.

Colobus wanted
a feathered cut
but he got stubble.

"Who's next?" she called, waving over Cockatoo, Cormorant and Crane.

Holly the hairdresser was in full swing. She herded Lion, Flamingo, Moose and Bear from the hair washing area to be blow dried. She volumised Lion's mane, fluffed Flamingo up to three times her size, moussed Moose and backcombed Bear.

"There! All finished!" she said, clapping her hands delightedly, just as …

... Herbert hopped up the steps from the back of the salon. "What HAVE you done!" cried Herbert. "You bad, bad hare."

Holly looked up at her Uncle
with sad, big brown eyes.
"I was only trying to help,"
she said, slipping
her paw into his.

At that moment the salon doors swung open.
"Darlings! Have you had a lovely time?"
Mama dropped her shopping.

Yummies

"Good heavens, Herbert!" she cried.
"Whatever's happened?"
Herbert looked down at Holly.
"Lets just say its been a
bad hare day," he said.

Chocolate
Herb Tea
Raspberry Milk
Coffee